Emily
Loves to
BOUNCE

For: Alethea, Ashleigh, Ciara, Imogen, Luka and Tanith.

Thanks to: Trish for sustaining the vision and Margaret Connolly for inspiring liberation.

First American Edition published in 2003 by Philomel Books,
a division of Penguin Putnam Books for Young Readers,
345 Hudson Street, New York, NY 10014.
Philomel Books, Reg. U.S. Pat. & Tm. Off.
Published in Australia by Scholastic Press.
Printed in Singapore by Tien Wah Press Pte Ltd.
The text is set in Pixie.
Stephen Michael King used ink and watercolors
for the illustrations in this book.
Library of Congress Cataloging-in-Publication Data
King, Stephen Michael. Emily loves to bounce / Stephen Michael King.
p. cm. Summary: A young girl enjoys bouncing
in many ways and in many places.
[1. Jumping—Fiction. 2. Play—Fiction. 3. Stories in rhyme.] I. Title.
PZ8.3.K5973 Em 2003 [Fic]—dc21 2002002531
ISBN 0-399-23886-7
1 3 5 7 9 10 8 6 4 2
First American Edition

Emily Loves to BOUNCE

BOING

Stephen Michael King

Philomel Books ~ New York

Emily

loves

to

bounce

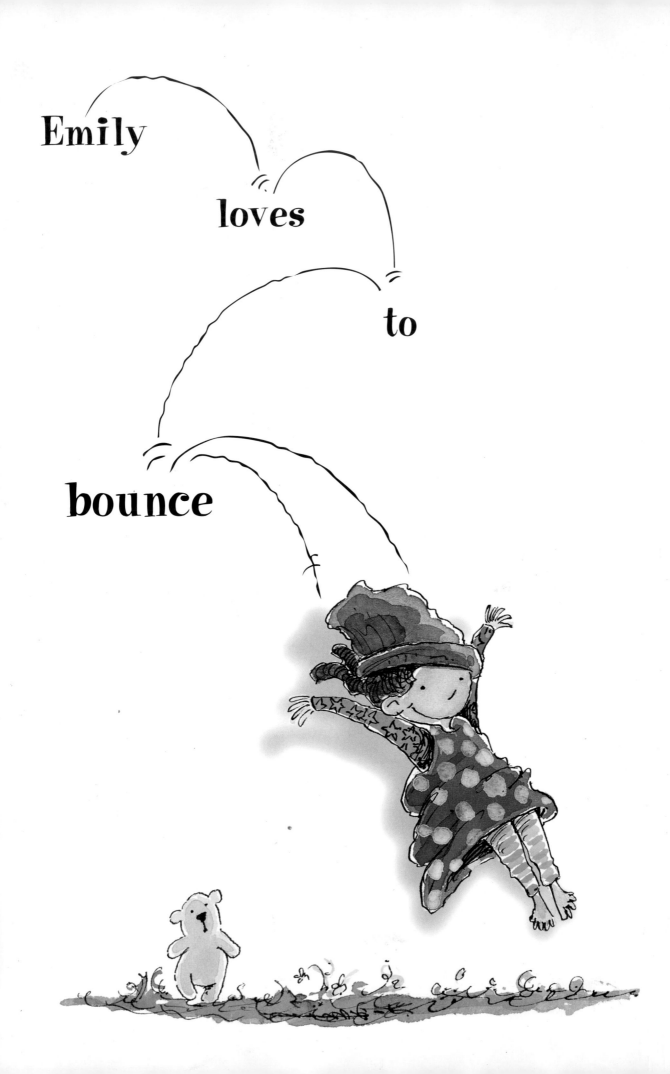

and bounce

and bounce

and bounce.

Sometimes she sleeps,

sometimes she eats,

but...

most of the time
she bounces.

High
bounces,

BOING

low bounces,

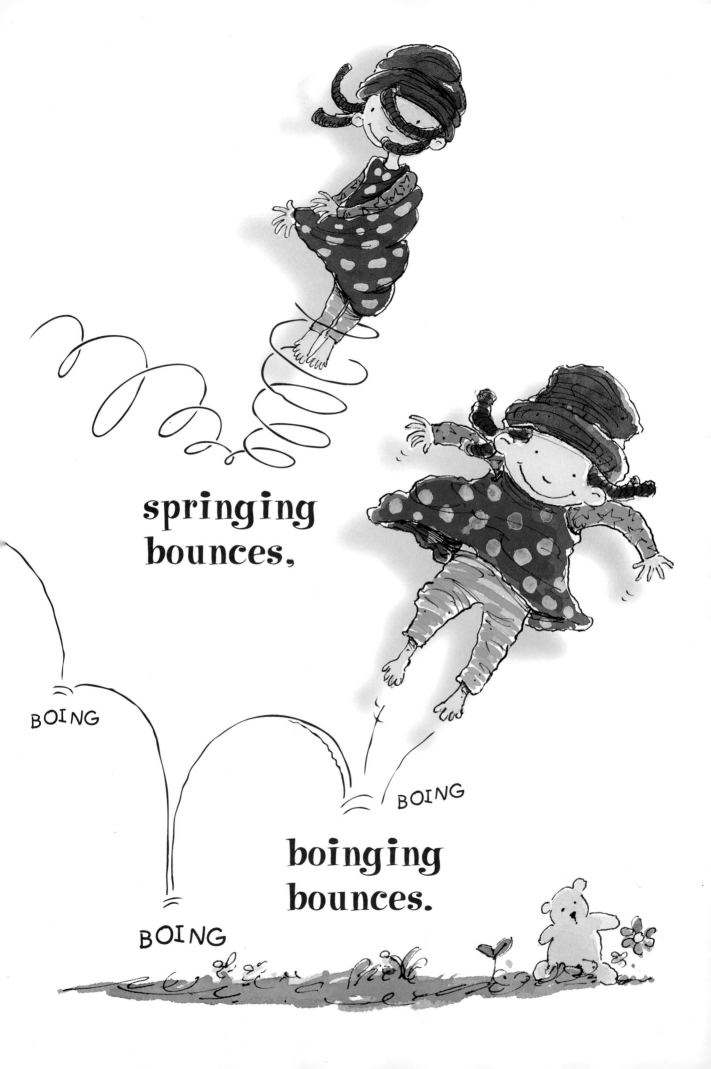

**springing
bounces,**

BOING

BOING

**boinging
bounces.**

BOING

Twisting,

toppling,

singing,

La la la

She can
flop on her
stomach bounce,

BOING

bounce
with her cat,

bounce with
an elephant,

boing on one
foot bounce,

and sit on her
bottom bounce.

She can bounce
with her dinosaur,

**or with
Nana Pat.**

She can flutter
like a fairy...

BOING

...spring like a frog,

or
sometimes
imagine
she's
a
blue-
spotted
dog.

She likes to...

...bounce into the sandbox,

or bounce down the hall. . . .

but. . .

bouncing on
Mom and Dad's bed. . .

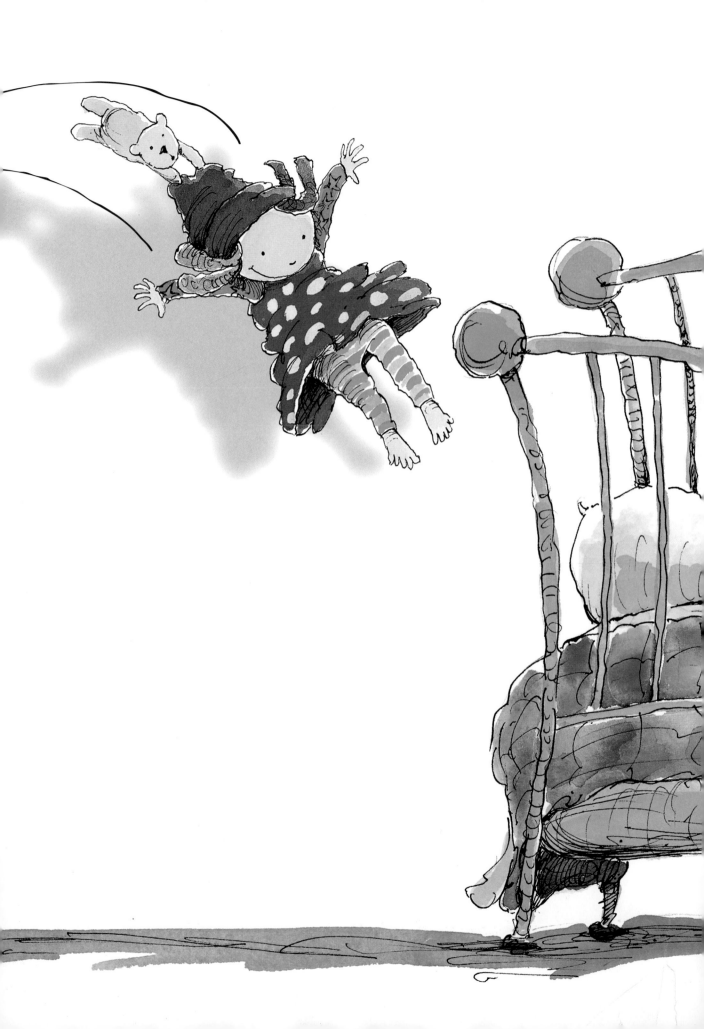

is the best bounce of all!